Also by Alvin Schwartz and Glen Rounds

CROSS YOUR FINGERS, SPIT IN YOUR HAT
Superstitions and Other Beliefs

TOMFOOLERY
Trickery and Foolery with Words

A TWISTER OF TWISTS, A TANGLER OF TONGUES

WHOPPERS
Tall Tales and Other Lies

WITCRACKS
Jokes and Jests from American Folklore

Other books by Alvin Schwartz

AND THE GREEN GRASS GREW ALL AROUND
Folk Poetry from Everyone

CHIN MUSIC
Tall Talk and Other Talk

FLAPDOODLE
Pure Nonsense from American Folklore

MORE SCARY STORIES TO TELL IN THE DARK

SCARY STORIES TO TELL IN THE DARK
Collected from American Folklore

SCARY STORIES 3
More Tales to Chill Your Bones

STORIES TO TELL A CAT

TELLING FORTUNES
Love Magic, Dream Signs, and Other Ways to Learn the Future

UNRIDDLING
All Sorts of Riddles to Puzzle Your Guessery, Collected from American Folklore

WHEN I GREW UP LONG AGO
People Talk About the Days When They Were Young

I Can Read Books®

ALL OF OUR NOSES ARE HERE And Other Noodle Tales

BUSY BUZZING BUMBLEBEES And Other Tongue Twisters

GHOSTS!: Ghostly Tales from Folklore

IN A DARK, DARK ROOM And Other Scary Stories

TEN COPYCATS IN A BOAT And Other Riddles

THERE IS A CARROT IN MY EAR And Other Noodle Tales

Kickle Snifters and other Fearsome Critters

Collected from American Folklore
by ALVIN SCHWARTZ
Illustrated by Glen Rounds

HarperTrophy
A Division of HarperCollins*Publishers*

Library of Congress Cataloging-in-Publication Data
Schwartz, Alvin, date
    Summary: Brief text and illustrations introduce such strange
creatures from American folklore as the snawfus, billdad,
lufferlang, and tripodero.
    1. Animals, Mythical—Juvenile literature.   2. Folklore—
United States—Juvenile literature.   [1. Folklore—United States.
2. Animals, Mythical]   I. Rounds, Glen, date   II. Title.
GR825.S37   1992   75-29048
398.24'5
ISBN 0-397-31645-3
ISBN 0-06-446129-7 (pbk.)

First Harper Trophy edition, 1992.

Table of Contents

*I*t is said that there are strange creatures all around us — in the woods, in the mountains, in the lakes, everywhere.

Cowboys, woodsmen, hunters, and other people see these creatures again and again. Or say they do. Here is what they tell of them.

snawfus

Just after the sun goes down look into the tree-tops. If you are lucky you will see a snawfus. A snawfus is a white deer with giant antlers from which flowers grow.

As it leaps from tree to tree it sings, "Halley-loo! Halley-loo!"

squonk

A squonk never sings. It is so upset by the way it looks, it cries all the time.

A famous hunter named Mule McSneed once
caught a squonk by following its teardrops. Then he

stuck it in a sack and took it home. But the squonk cried so hard that when he opened the sack nothing was left of it but a puddle.

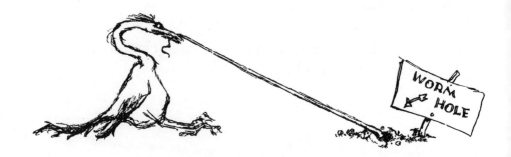

milamo bird

A milamo bird eats giant worms that live in giant wormholes. When it gets hungry *it* dives into one of these holes and finds itself a worm.

Then it pulls in one direction—and the worm pulls in the other. But each time it pulls, and each time the worm pulls, the worm stretches a little, like a rubber band.

When finally the worm is stretched too thin, it gives up and lets go. And it shoots out of its hole like a shot—and smacks the milamo between the eyes. Then it jumps back into its hole.

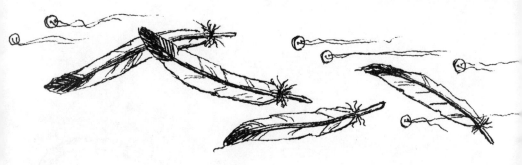

goofus bird

The goofus bird likes to see where it has been, not where it is going. So it flies backward. It also likes to sleep upside down. So it builds its nest bottom-side up.

billdad

If you walk along the shore of a big lake, and you don't make any noise, you may meet a billdad. For that is where it waits and watches for fish to jump from the water. When a billdad sees a fish, it leaps through the air and lands next to it. Then it smacks it with its tail . . . and carries it home and cooks it over a fire.

rubberado

A rubberado cannot leap or fly, or jump or climb, or swim or swing, or walk or run, or creep or crawl at all. It bounces from place to place. And each time it lands, it laughs.

The rubberado also makes a tasty stew, but do not eat any. If you do, you will bounce and laugh and bounce and laugh and bounce and laugh for days and days.

hugag

The hugag has no knees. Because of this it cannot sit down or lie down. (Keep your legs stiff, and you will see what a problem this is.) When a hugag sleeps, it must lean against a tree or a house or a fence. But it is so big and so heavy it causes whatever it leans against to bend.

If you see a tree or a house or a fence that leans to one side, a hugag slept there.

splinter cat

A splinter cat eats wild bees which live in the trunks of trees. At mealtime it climbs to the top of the tallest tree it can find. Then it dives face first into the trunk of a tree nearby...

and smashes it to smithereens. If there are no bees inside, it tries another tree and another and another. Most people think storms destroy these trees. But they are wrong.

timberdoodle

If a timberdoodle bites you, be patient. It will not let go until it hears the sound of thunder. Once a timberdoodle bit Mule McSneed, and it took him two months to get away.

hide-behind

When a woodsman or a hunter enters the deepest woods and does not come back, most people say he got lost. But some say a hide-behind that hid behind a tree grabbed him.

windigo

Others say a windigo did, a shadowy creature
with a voice like the moaning of the wind and
big feet.

tree-squeak

When you are in the woods and you hear a

> *squeaky, screechy screech*
> or a
> *screechy, squeaky screech*
> or a
> *screechy, squeaky squeak*
> or a
> *squeaky, screechy squeak,*

what you hear is a tree-squeak. But it is hard to see, for its skin is covered with bark just like the bark that covers its tree.

lufferlang

If you live where lufferlangs do, carry a big mirror at all times. Then if a lufferlang attacks, hold the mirror in front of you. For what frightens it most is seeing itself.

31

side-hill gouger

A side-hill gouger lives on a mountain peak and eats rocks. But what is peculiar about this animal is its legs.

Its uphill legs are much shorter than its downhill legs. This gives it a good foothold, which keeps it from falling off the mountain.

When it tries to turn around, however, these legs never are where they should be. And it loses its balance and tumbles into the valley below.

If a gouger has any brains, it never turns around. It walks around and around its mountain in the same direction all of its life. Of course, young gougers complain that they never go *anyplace*. But where could they go?

glyptodont

A glyptodont has on its chest a pouch in which it carries rocks. Each day after lunch it pulls one out and places it on a boulder. Then it spins around, faster and faster, until you can hardly see it. Then with its tail it whacks the rock at a tree.

If the rock hits the tree, the glyptodont jumps for joy. But if it misses, it pounds its tail on the ground and howls with anger and cries like a baby.

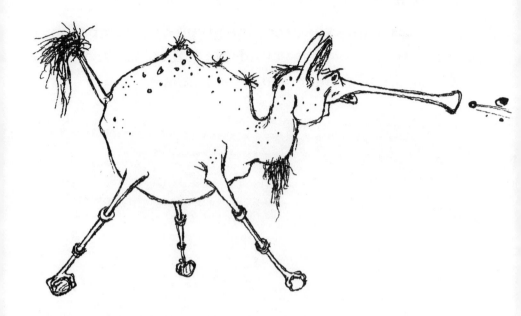

tripodero

A tripodero moves up and down like an elevator. When its enemies are near, it shrinks its legs to nothing and hides. But when it hunts, it travels on legs ten feet long.

In each cheek it carries a pound of pebbles it fires through its snout. If you see a tripodero, stay out of sight. It might fire them at you.

slide-rock bolter

A slide-rock bolter hangs by its tail from a mountain peak for days on end, looking for something to eat. When finally it sees a spider far below — spiders are what bolters like best — it very carefully aims itself and zooms down...

and gobbles it up.

gowrow

The gowrow is so enormous, the earth shakes when it walks. It hatches from an egg and lives in a cave and shrieks "Gow-row! Gow-row!" which is why it is called that.

Sometimes people at a carnival pay fifty cents to see a gowrow.

They go into a darkened tent and wait for a curtain to be pulled back. Soon there is a terrible roar and screams and gunshots. And a man rushes out and shouts, "The gowrow is loose! Run for your lives!"

And everybody runs. But if *you* are there, don't you run, not until you get your money back. For this is an old trick to cheat people.

There is no gowrow behind that curtain. There is only an old woman roaring and screaming and banging on a pan and firing a gun in the air.

jump-at-a-body

When you least expect it, a jump-at-a-body will jump from behind a tree, then charge at you like an angry lion, then stop short and run away.

wunk

Whenever a wunk sees anybody or anything, it digs a hole,
    and jumps in,
    and pulls the hole in after it.

Of course, a wunk doesn't have to hide in a hole. If it wanted to, it could turn itself into a real person, into somebody that looks like you or like me, and walk around town and do all kinds of things. But it doesn't want to.

squidgicum-squee

This animal is just as shy as
the wunk. But when *it* sees
anybody or anything, it
takes a deep breath
and swallows
itself.

A writer named James Whitcomb Riley once wrote a poem he called "The Raggedy Man." Part of it tells about the wunk and the squidgicum-squee. It goes like this:

An' The Raggedy Man, he knows most rhymes,
An' tells 'em, ef I be good, sometimes;
Knows about Giunts, an' Griffins, an' Elves,
An' the Squidgicum-Squees 'at swallers the're-
    selves;
An', wite by the pump in our pasture-lot,
He showed me the hole 'at the Wunks is got,
'At lives way deep in the ground, an' can
Turn into me, 'er Lizabuth Ann!
Er Ma, er Pa, er The Raggedy Man!

But you ought to read the whole thing. It's a good poem.

whing-whang

On nights when the moon is a giant orange in the sky, the whing-whang leaps about the beach and with its tail writes *whing-whang, whing-whang, whing-whang* in the sand. But when the moon goes down and the sun comes up, it rubs out what it has written and disappears.

hoopajuba

This is a fish very few people have caught. But you could catch one. Just follow these simple directions:

1. Row to the center of a deep lake.

2. Drill a hole in the bottom of the lake, for that is where hoopajubas live.

3. Row back to shore and hide.

4. Make a sound like a mudworm, for that is what hoopajubas eat.

5. Wait quietly.

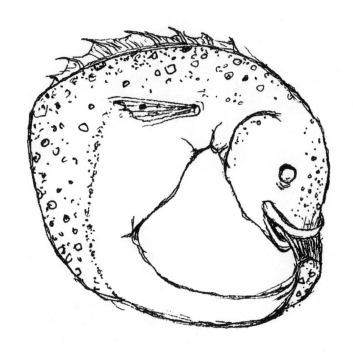

When a hoopajuba hears the sound of a mudworm, it will swim as fast as it can to the beach. Then it will put its tail in its mouth and roll toward the worm, that is, toward *you*. When it gets close enough, stick your hand through the hoop and drop the "hoopa" in your fishing basket.

hoop snake

The hoop snake also rolls like a hoop. But it carries on its tail a fang filled with the deadliest poison. Years ago a hoop snake chased Mule McSneed all morning, then finally cornered him and reared back to strike.

But Mule jumped aside, and the snake hit a tree with its deadly fang and filled *it* with poison instead. By the next day that tree had swelled so much it was as fat as a school bus.

Since Mule's cows needed a new shed, he cut the tree into boards and built them one. Then a strange thing happened.

As the poison in the wood dried out, the swelling in the boards went down. And the boards got smaller and smaller, and the shed got smaller and smaller, and the cows got more and more crowded — until one day that shed was no bigger than a doghouse.

So Mule moved his cows out and his dogs in, but he was mighty disappointed. And so were his cows.

If a hoop snake ever chases you, just dive through its hoop, and it will race away. But Mule McSneed did not know that.

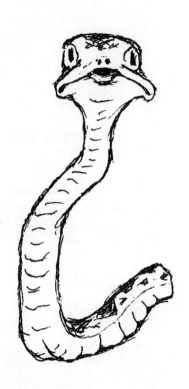

joint snake

When it is in danger, the joint snake breaks into a dozen pieces. Then each piece wiggles off in a different direction. When the coast is clear, the pieces come out of hiding and hook together and go on their way.

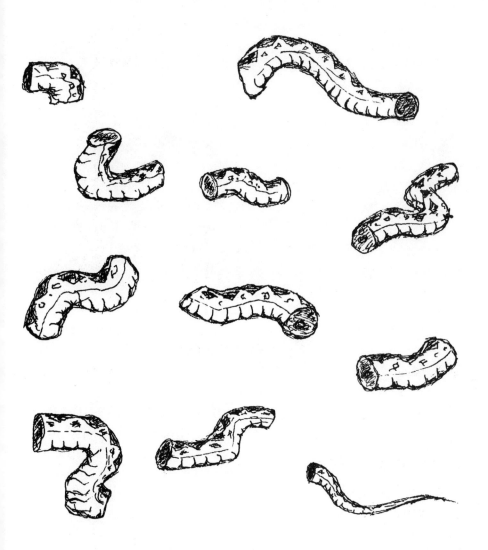

sea serpent

This sea serpent is about three hundred feet long. When it came ashore a professor who was picking beach plums on the beach hid in the bushes and watched.

First the serpent took a drink of fresh water at a pond nearby. Then it stared for a minute at the sea and whispered, "See you soon, sea. See you soon," and headed into the countryside. Nobody has seen it since.

kickle snifters

Kickle snifters are about the size of your thumb. They live inside old men's beards. But this gets boring, and they are forever peeking out. They also are forever laughing, because beard hair tickles.

You are most likely to see kickle snifters at your grandfather's house, or your great-uncle's house, when you have eaten too much supper, and you begin to feel sleepy, and your eyes try to close, and things don't look the way they usually do.

Pranking the Tenderfoot

The creatures in this bestiary live only in our imaginations.

A few were born in the work of James Whitcomb Riley. Others emerged from the light, shadow, and sound of a lonely wood. Others are straight-out lies, cousins to the tall tale, spun by frontiersmen, woodsmen, cowboys, and carnival sharps to prank the tenderfoot and pass the time.

All are part of an unnatural history that reaches back to our earliest mythology.

Folklorists classify our folk animals as "fearsome critters," although most are funny, not fearsome. One scholar has placed the number of distinct species identified as eighty-one. But clearly there are more. The next time you are in the woods or anywhere, look closely and listen carefully and you may see one.

NOTES AND SOURCES

See Bibliography for information on sources. Except for a passage from "The Raggedy Man," all references have been adapted and many have been embellished.

Snawfus, Randolph, 49. One variety exhales blue smoke which produces an autumn haze in the Ozark Mountains. *Squonk*, Cox, 31. Similar to whang-doodle, Mencken, 251. *Milamo*, Boatright, 29. *Goofus bird*, general. Also fillyloo crane, filla-ma-loo bird, bogie bird. Related to the sand hill perch found in dry desert streams which swims backward to keep dust out of its eyes, Davidson, 283. *Billdad*, Cox 43. *Rubberado*, MacDougall, 14, 24. *Hugag*, Cox, 9. *Splinter cat*, Cox 37. *Timberdoodle*, Tyron, x. *Hide-behind*, general. Also high-behind. *Windigo*, Skinner, 37. *Tree-squeak*, general. *Lufferlang*, Botkin quoting Brown, 645; reference to mirror, Tyron, 31. *Side-hill gouger*, general. So named for the path it gouges in mountainsides. Also side-hill dodger, hoofer, and wowser; gwinter, guyiscutus, prock, and yam-hill lunkus. Cows and milking stools of similar construction have been reported. Also see Mencken, 245-248. *Glyptodont*, Boatright, 34; Randolph, 51. Also hinge-tailed bingbuffer. *Tripodero*, general. First sighted after invention of telescoping legs. *Slide-rock bolter*, Cox, 21. *Gowrow*, Randolph, 43. *Carnival trick*, general. *Jump-at-a-body*, general. Also come-at-a-body, Tyron, 13. *Wunk, Squidgicum-squee*, "The Raggedy Man," Riley, 462-463. *Whing-whang*, Riley, 450. *Hoopajuba*, Peach, 18. Similar to whifflepoodle, Boatright, 31-34. *Hoop snake, shrinking house tale*, general.

Because of a horny growth on its tail, the red-bellied snake, *Farancia abacuram*, is regarded by some as a hoop snake. In all cases the hoop snake is reputed to develop its momentum by rolling downhill. *Joint snake*, general. *Sea serpent*, general. For account of serpent described, Skinner, 280-281. *Kickle snifter*, "Fields for Collectors," 188. Also kickle swifter, hickle snifter.

BIBLIOGRAPHY

Boatright, Mody C. *Tall Tales from Texas Cow Camps*. Dallas: Southwest Press, 1934. Botkin, B.A., ed. *A Treasury of American Folklore*. New York: Crown Publishers, Inc., 1944. Brown, C.E. *Paul Bunyan Natural History*. Madison, Wis.: C.E. Brown, 1935. Cox, William T. *Fearsome Critters of the Lumberwoods, with a Few Desert and Mountain Beasts*. Washington, D.C.: Press of Judd & Detweiler, Inc., 1910. Davidson, Levette J., and Blake, Forrester, eds. *Rocky Mountain Tales*. Norman, Okla.: University of Oklahoma Press, 1947. "Fearsome Critters." *Standard Dictionary of Folklore, Mythology and Legend*. Edited by Maria Leach. New York: Funk & Wagnalls Publishing Co., 1972. "Fields for Collectors," *Dialect Notes 5* (1922): 188. "Hoop snake," Connecticut Folklore Studies, W 3351. WPA Folklore Archives, 1936. Krapp, George P. *The English Language in America*. 2 vol. New York: The Century Company, 1925. MacDougall, Curtis D. *Hoaxes*. New York: Dover Publications, Inc., 1958. Masterson, James R. "Travelers' Tales of Colonial Natural History," *Journal of American Folklore 59* (1946): 174-188, 510-567. Mencken, H. L. *The American Language*, Supp.I. New York: Alfred A. Knopf, 1945. Miller, William M. "Another Hoopsnake Story," *Journal of American Folklore 64* (1961): 423. Peach, Arthur W. "A Creel of Big Ones," *New York Times Magazine*, April 11, 1948, p. 18. Penn, A. W. "Tall Tales for the Tenderfoot," *Texas Folklore Society Publication 7* (1928): 38-41. Randolph, Vance. *We Always Lie to Strangers: Tall Tales from the Ozarks*. New York: Columbia University Press, 1951. Riley, James Whitcomb. *Complete Poetical Works of James Whitcomb Riley*. New York: Grossett & Dunlap, 1937. "Sidehill Gougers," Oregon Folklore Studies, W 9681. WPA Folklore Archives, 1939. Skinner, Charles M. *American Myths and Legends*, Vol. 1 Philadelphia and London: J.B. Lippincott Company, 1903. Tyron, Henry H. *Fearsome Critters*. Cornwall, N.Y.: Idlewild Press, 1939.